It is sunny and Bee, Snake, and Inky have had a picnic.

Snake is asleep and snoring. He has had lots of egg sandwiches.

Bee and Inky are in the forest. They are looking for interesting things.

Under the ground is a big ants' nest. The ants are all rushing about.

They can smell something sweet and sticky. Jam!

They come up to the top of the ant hill and look around.

They see Snake asleep in the sun. They see the picnic things. They see the jam.

The ants collect the jam jar and march back to the ant hill with it.

Bee and Inky come back from the forest. They have found lots of interesting things.

Snake sits up and looks at the things they have found: sweet chestnuts, some twigs, and a bit of bark.

It will be dark soon.

Snake, Bee, and Inky start to pack up the picnic things.

They look and look but they cannot see the jar of jam.

Under the ground, in the ants' nest, the ants are happy.

They have lots of jam for dinner!